THOMAS & FRIENDS™

Gordon

Based on
The Railway Series
by the
Rev. W. Awdry

Illustrations by
Robin Davies

EGMONT

This story is about Gordon the Big Engine, Sodor's fastest engine! Gordon always thinks he knows best, but when things go wrong, he doesn't feel quite so grand . . .

Big blue Gordon loved showing off and telling the other engines what to do.

"Watch me rush past with the Express this afternoon," he said to Edward. "It will be such a splendid sight!"

"And please don't bump your trucks," Gordon went on. "Really Useful Engines **never** do that."

Then Gordon steamed away.

Edward didn't listen to Gordon.

He was having too much fun bumping his train of trucks. **BIFF!**

"Ouch!" cried the trucks. "What's going on?"

Just then, Edward heard a long whistle. **"Pooop!"**

It was Gordon, looking cross. He wasn't pulling the shiny Express coaches.

"Dirty coal trucks," moaned Gordon. "Oh, the indignity!"

Gordon rumbled by with the trucks **click-clacking** behind. Edward smiled.

Then there was trouble.

A Porter came and spoke to Edward's Driver. "Gordon can't get up the hill. We need Edward's help!" he said.

Halfway up the hill, Edward found that Gordon had stopped.

"These silly trucks won't go," groaned Gordon.

Edward rolled up behind Gordon's brake van.

"You'll be no use," huffed Gordon.
"Wait and see," Edward replied.

The Guard blew his whistle. Gordon pulled and
Edward pushed.

"I can't do it, I can't do it," Gordon wheezed.
"Yes you can, yes you can," Edward called.

Edward **pushed** and **puffed** with all his strength until Gordon reached the top of the hill.

"I've done it!" smiled Gordon. The big engine steamed on to the next station without stopping to say thank you to Edward.

The Fat Controller didn't forget to thank Edward. The next day, Edward was given a shiny new coat of blue paint with red stripes.

Gordon hadn't learnt his lesson. He still thought he was better than the other engines.

"Henry, you whistle too much," said Gordon, one night. "Really Useful Engines **never** whistle loudly. Not on The Fat Controller's Railway."

Henry felt sad.

"I like your whistling, Henry!" whispered Percy.

The next day, Henry and Edward suddenly heard an engine's whistle, getting louder and louder.

"It sounds like Gordon," gasped Henry. "But it can't be!"

It **was** Gordon! His safety valve wouldn't close and he was whistling fit to burst! He raced through the station at a tremendous speed.

Henry smiled. "Really Useful Engines **never** whistle loudly," he said.

"POOOOOOP!"

What a terrible sound! The passengers and crew covered their ears as Gordon **screeched** along. So did The Fat Controller.

"Take him away," The Fat Controller boomed. "And stop that noise!"

Still whistling, Gordon **wheeshed** away.

Gordon **whistled** as he crossed the points.
He **whistled** in the siding. He was still **whistling** as the last passenger left the station!

Then two Engineers climbed up and knocked Gordon's whistle valve shut. At last, the whistling stopped.

Gordon puffed slowly to the Sheds.

That night, the other engines couldn't help but tease Gordon.

"Really Useful Engines **never** whistle loudly," said Henry quietly. "Not on this Railway!"

All the other engines laughed, except Gordon.

From then on, Gordon was a quieter, wiser engine — well, for a few days, anyway!

More about Gordon

funnel

dome

boiler bands

tender

buffer

coupling rod

coupling hook

• Gordon's challenge to you •

Look back through the pages of this book
and see if you can spot:

fire engine

dog

whistle

poppies

moon

  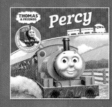